Triceratops for Lunch

Adapted by Andrea Posner-Sanchez
Based on the television series created by Craig Bartlett
Illustrated by Caleb Meurer

A GOLDEN BOOK • NEW YORK

TM & © 2010 The Jim Henson Company. JIM HENSON'S mark & logo, DINOSAUR TRAIN mark & logo, characters and elements are trademarks of The Jim Henson Company. All Rights Reserved. Published in the United States by Golden Books, an imprint of Random House Children's Books, a division of Random House, Inc., 1745 Broadway, New York, NY 10019, and in Canada by Random House of Canada Limited, Toronto. Golden Books, A Golden Book, A Little Golden Book, the G colophon, and the distinctive gold spine are registered trademarks of Random House, Inc.
www.randomhouse.com/kids
Library of Congress Control Number: 2009938959
ISBN: 978-0-375-86151-2
Printed in the United States of America
10 9 8 7 6 5 4

Buddy, Shiny, Tiny, and Don are heading home to help their mother clean their nest. They are having company!

"Who's coming over?" Buddy asks.

"I don't know," says Tiny, "but I bet they're coming for lunch, and that means we're having fish!"

Like all Pteranodons, Shiny, Tiny, and Don love fish. They eat it all the time. In fact, they even sing a song about it.

"If I could wish for just one dish, my greatest wish would be more **FISH!!!**"

Their brother Buddy is a different kind of dinosaur.
He doesn't love fish as much as they do.
"Um . . . does anyone else ever get a little tired
of fish?" he asks.
    Tiny, Shiny, and Don can't believe their ears!

Mrs. Pteranodon explains that some dinosaurs don't like fish at all. "Herbivores are dinosaurs that only eat plants," she tells her children. "We are carnivores. We eat meat. Fish is meat."

Later, Mrs. Pteranodon, Buddy, Tiny, and Don go
to the Dinosaur Train Station to meet their guests.
But Don doesn't know what a Triceratops looks like.

TRICERATOPS

Triceratops have three horns.

1
2
3

They walk on four legs.

1 2 3 4

They have the biggest head of any creature on earth!

"Kids, this is Trudy Triceratops and her son, Tank," Mrs. Pteranodon says as she welcomes her friend.

The kids greet each other.

"High four!"
says Tank.

"High three!"
says Tiny.

"High two!"
adds Buddy
with a laugh.

Don is too amazed by Tank's big head to join in.

"So, Tank, what sounds more delicious: fish or plants?" Tiny asks.

"Plants!" Tank answers right away. "I'm an herbivore. To me, plants are the best food ever!"

Mrs. Pteranodon is happy to know what to serve
her friends for lunch.

But when the two families arrive back at the nest,
it seems Shiny has other plans.

"Ta-daah! Fish!" she announces.

"I don't eat fish," Tank says.

"Fish is your favorite food—you just don't know it yet!" Shiny tells the Triceratops.

Tank is so hungry he agrees to try it.

"Blech!" he declares as he spits the fish out.

Trudy explains that Triceratops' beaks are not made to eat fish. They are perfect for chomping through thick, tough plants.

Tank shows everyone how his beak works by happily eating a whole bush in no time at all.

"Let's ride the Dinosaur Train to the Big Pond,"
Buddy suggests. "Tank can eat all he wants over
there."

On board, Mr. Conductor stops by with the snack
cart. He has lots of yummy-looking leafy treats.
But Trudy doesn't want Tank to ruin his appetite
before lunch.

As soon as they get to the Big Pond, Tank starts eating. He uses his super sharp beak to yank down leaves and chew them up.

"I don't understand," Shiny says. "I have a beak, too, but I don't like leaves at all."

Shiny's beak is long and thin. Tank's beak is short and thick.

Tank has hundreds of teeth. Shiny doesn't have any teeth at all.

Buddy has teeth, too, but they look different from Tank's.

"Maybe *I'm* an herbivore!" Buddy declares. He eats some leaves. They're hard to chew and don't taste very good. "Oh, well, I'll just keep trying new things until I figure out what I like best!"

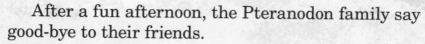

After a fun afternoon, the Pteranodon family say good-bye to their friends.

"You sure you don't want to try a leafwich? Or a dipped leaf cluster?" Tank yells to Buddy.

"No leaves for me," Buddy responds. "Bye!"

Back at home, Don pretends to be a Triceratops. "I'll eat all the leaves in the world!" he bellows as he munches on a plant. "Ugh! Leaves taste awful!"

Tiny, Shiny, and Buddy laugh. "Not if you're an herbivore!" says Tiny.